DARK MAN

THE DARK CANDLE

by Peter Lancett

illustrated by Jan Pedroietta

SADDLEBACK
EDUCATIONAL PUBLISHING

DARK MAN

The Dark Candle
The Dark Machine
The Dark Words
The Day is Dark
Dying for the Dark
Killer in the Dark

© Ransom Publishing Ltd. 2007

Text © Peter Lancett 2007

Illustrations © Jan Pedroietta 2007

David Strachan, The Old Man and The Shadow Masters appear
by kind permission of Peter Lancett

This edition is published by arrangement with Ransom Publishing Ltd.

SADDLEBACK
EDUCATIONAL PUBLISHING
www.sdlback.com

ISBN-13: 978-1-61651-026-8
ISBN-10: 1-61651-026-9

Printed in Guangzhou, China
0510/05-78-10

15 14 13 12 11   1 2 3 4 5

Chapter One:
A Great Power

The Old Man comes to the bad part of the city to see the Dark Man.

With him is a girl in her late teens.

The Dark Man knows her. She has helped him and the Old Man more than once.

"Take her to find the Dark Candle," the Old Man says, looking at the girl.

"She is very sick. Even our magic cannot help her. But the Dark Candle can make her well."

"What does it do?" the Dark Man asks.

"It gives people what they need," the Old Man replies. "If health is what someone needs, it gives health."

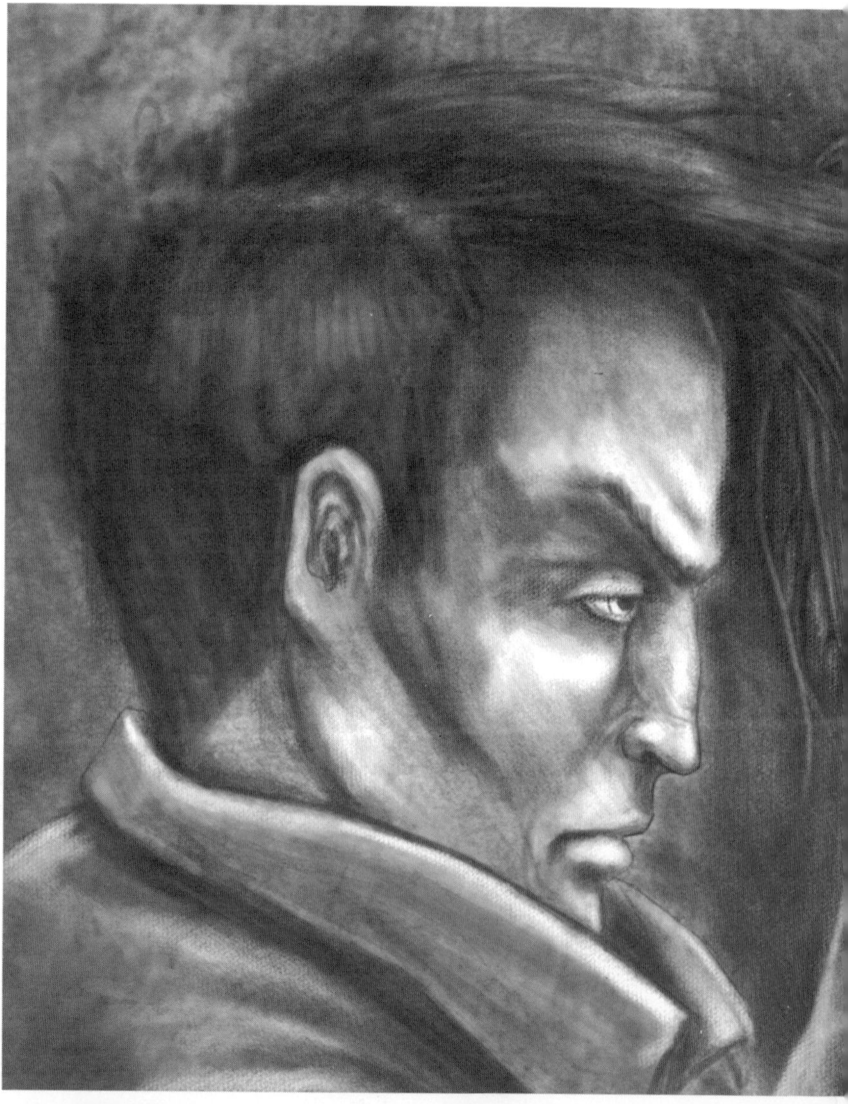

"That is a great power," the Dark Man says.

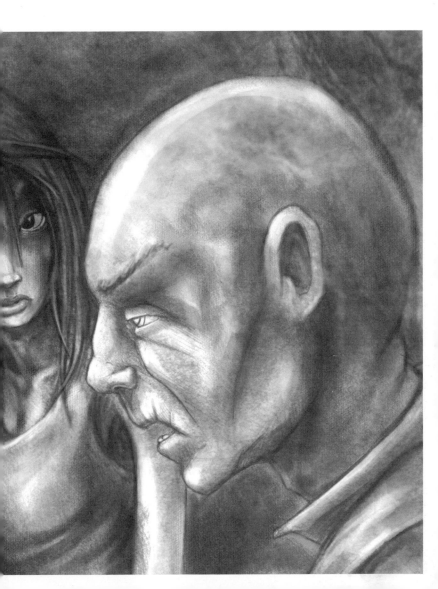

"The Dark Candle can also see through lies," the Old Man continues.

"It sees what you truly need, not what you simply want."

Chapter Two:
Black Clouds

Three days later, the Dark Man is sitting in a cave near the ocean.

It is cold. The sky outside is gray.

Next to him, the girl lies sleeping. She presses closer to him for warmth, then she begins to stir.

As he looks at her, the Dark Man is sad. She is lovely, but her sickness is killing her. She gets tired very easily, but she is very brave.

"Do you think the Dark Candle is near here?" the girl asks.

"Yes," the Dark Man replies. "I think so."

He takes some food from his shoulder bag.

"Here, you need to eat."

"No," the girl says. "Let's move on. I'm ready."

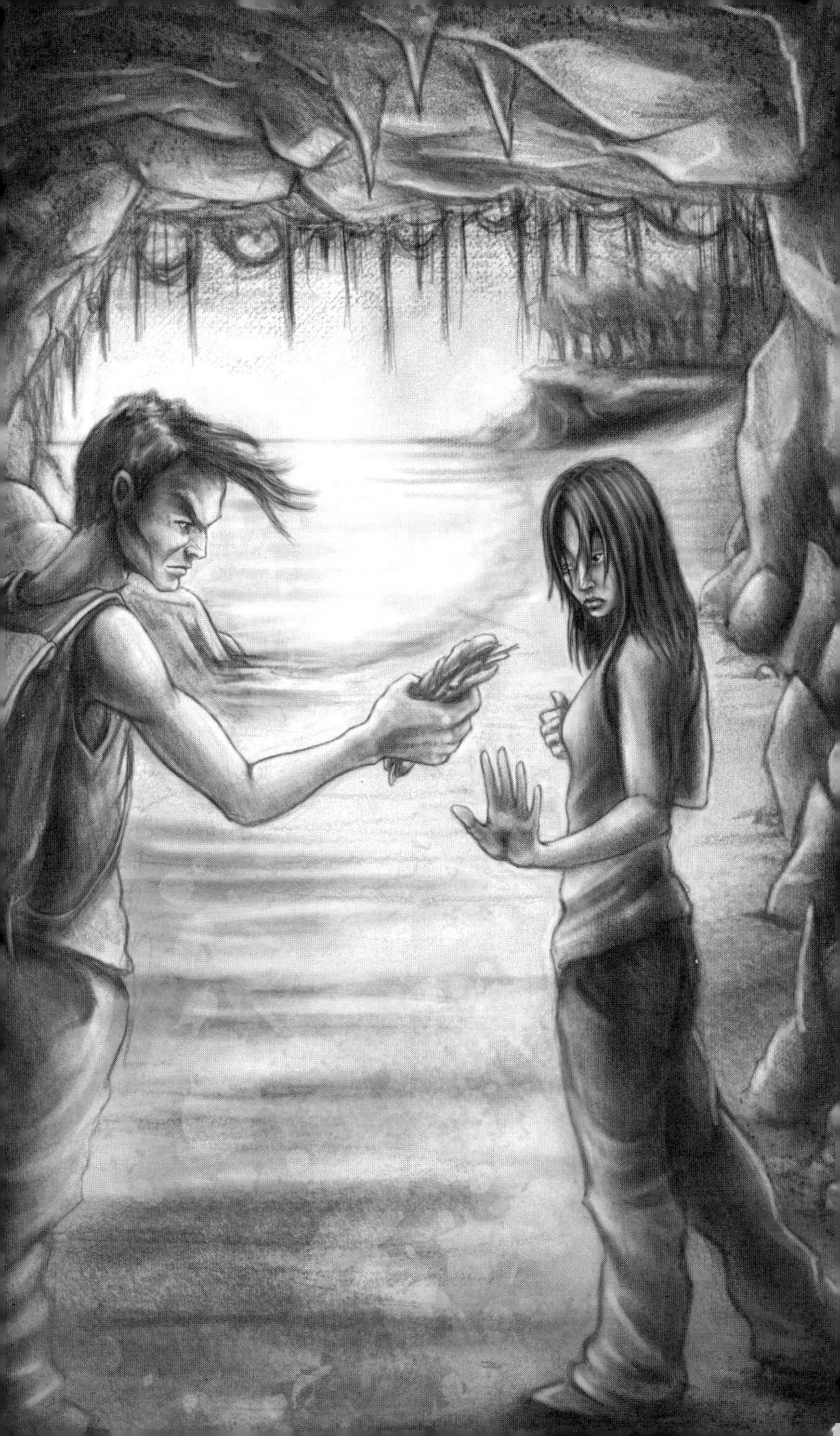

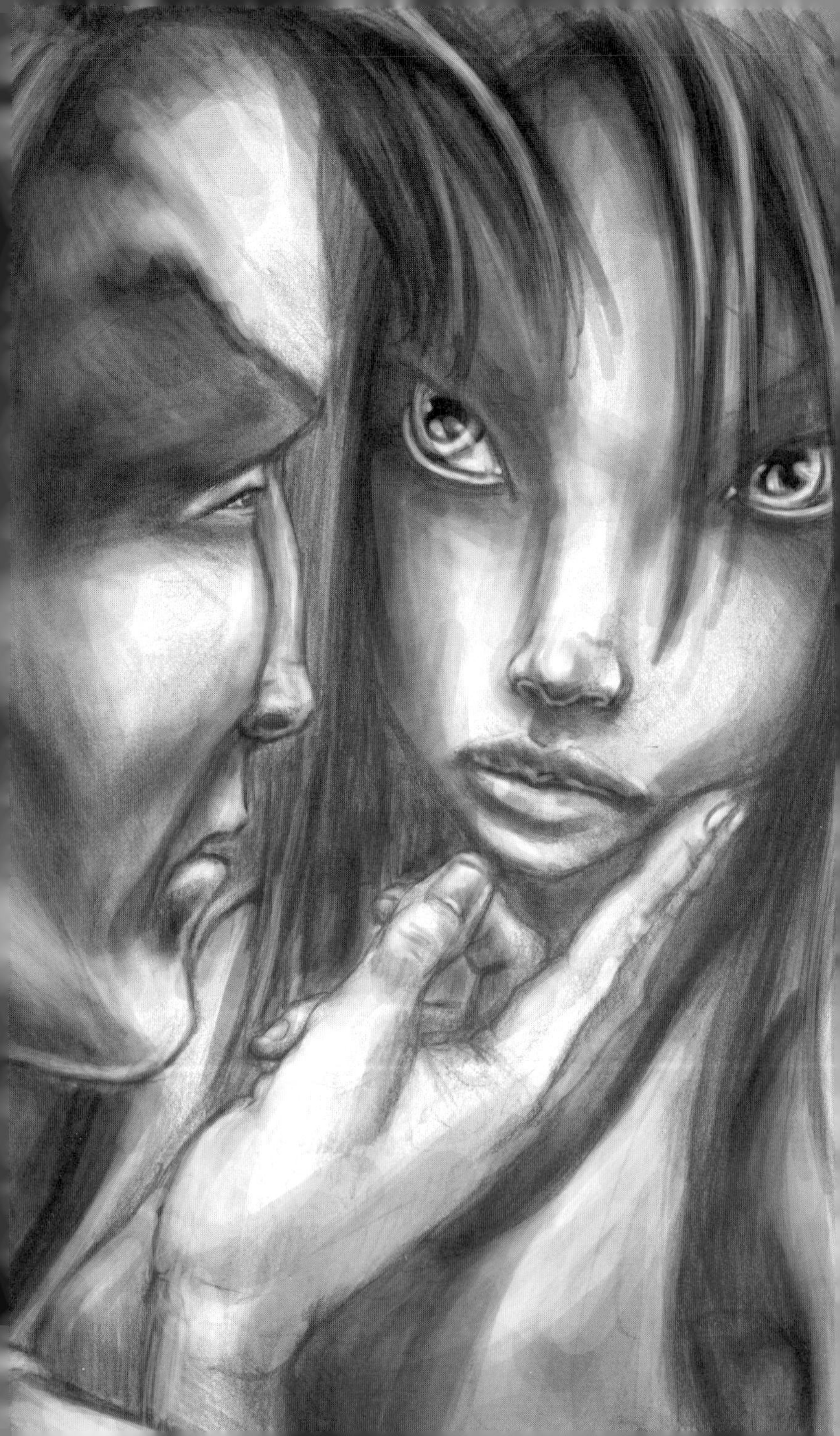

The Dark Man strokes her cheek gently. "Eat first," he says. "Food will give you strength."

In the afternoon, they are walking along the beach. Tall cliffs rise above them.

They have walked all morning, stopping often to let the girl rest. She is weary, but she never complains.

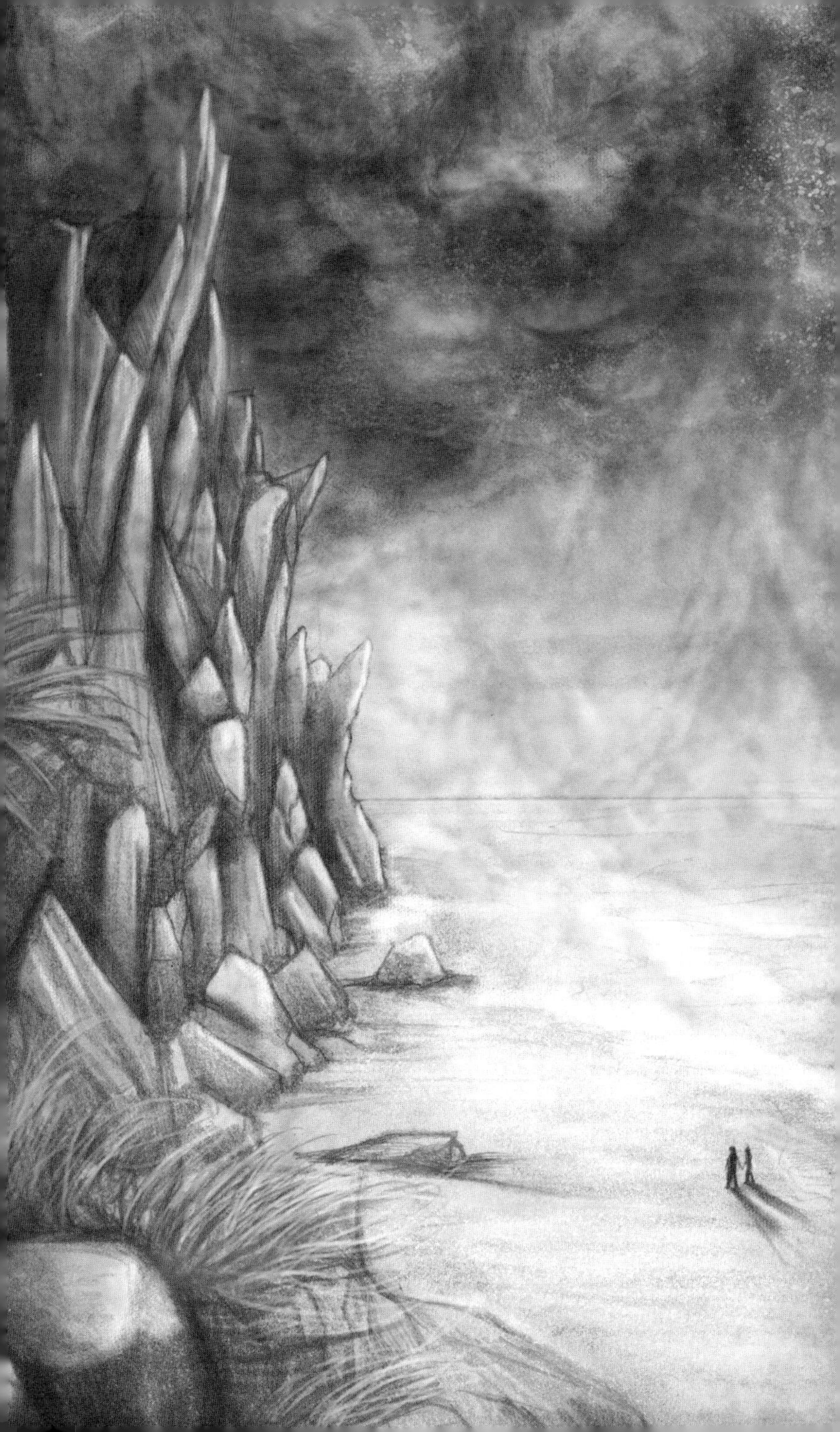

The Dark Man sees a large rock nearby.

"Come on, we can rest for a minute," he says.

"We don't have to," the girl replies. "I can keep going."

The Dark Man takes her hand and leads her to the rock.

"Just for a minute," he says. "We have time for that."

As they sit, the girl leans against the Dark Man's shoulder.

Soon, she is sleeping.

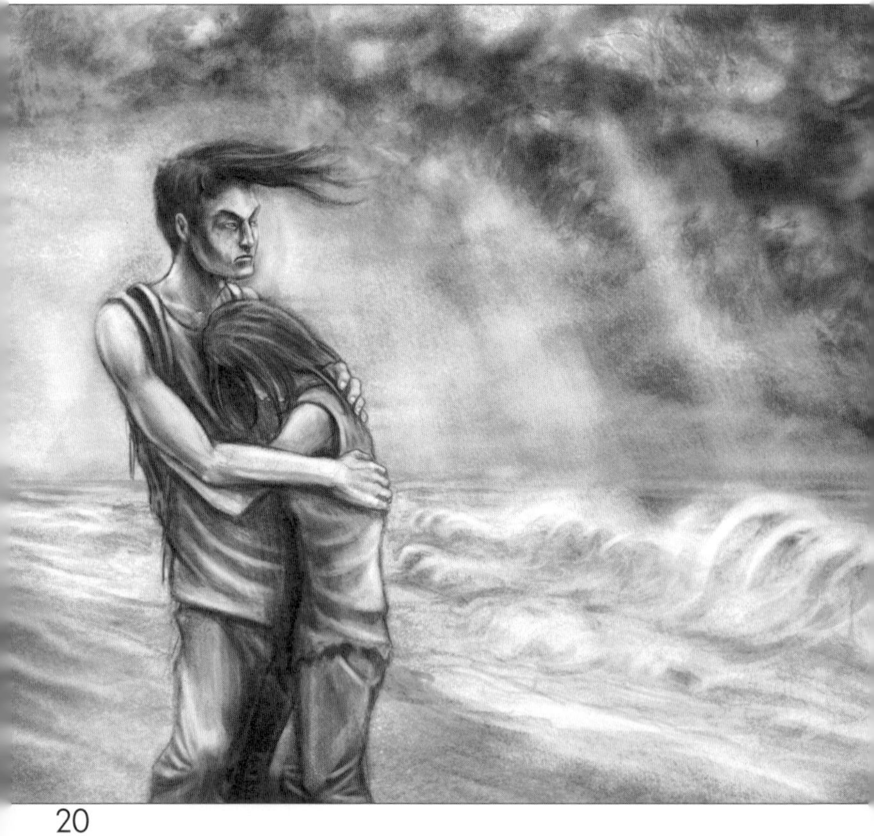

The Dark Man looks out to sea.

As he watches, the clouds grow blacker and the waves grow bigger, crashing against the shore.

A harsh wind blows.

Next to the Dark Man, the girl stirs.

"Is it night?" she asks. "How long did I sleep?"

"Only a minute or two," the Dark Man tells her. "The clouds make it seem like night."

The Dark Man is alert. The weather has changed too quickly.

He looks around and sees a gray figure dart behind a rock, some distance away. Someone is following them.

"Come on," the Dark Man says to the girl. "We should go, before the weather gets worse."

Chapter Three:
The Hermit

He helps her to her feet, but she stumbles.

Over her shoulder, the Dark Man sees the shadowy figure hide behind a rock. The figure is much closer now.

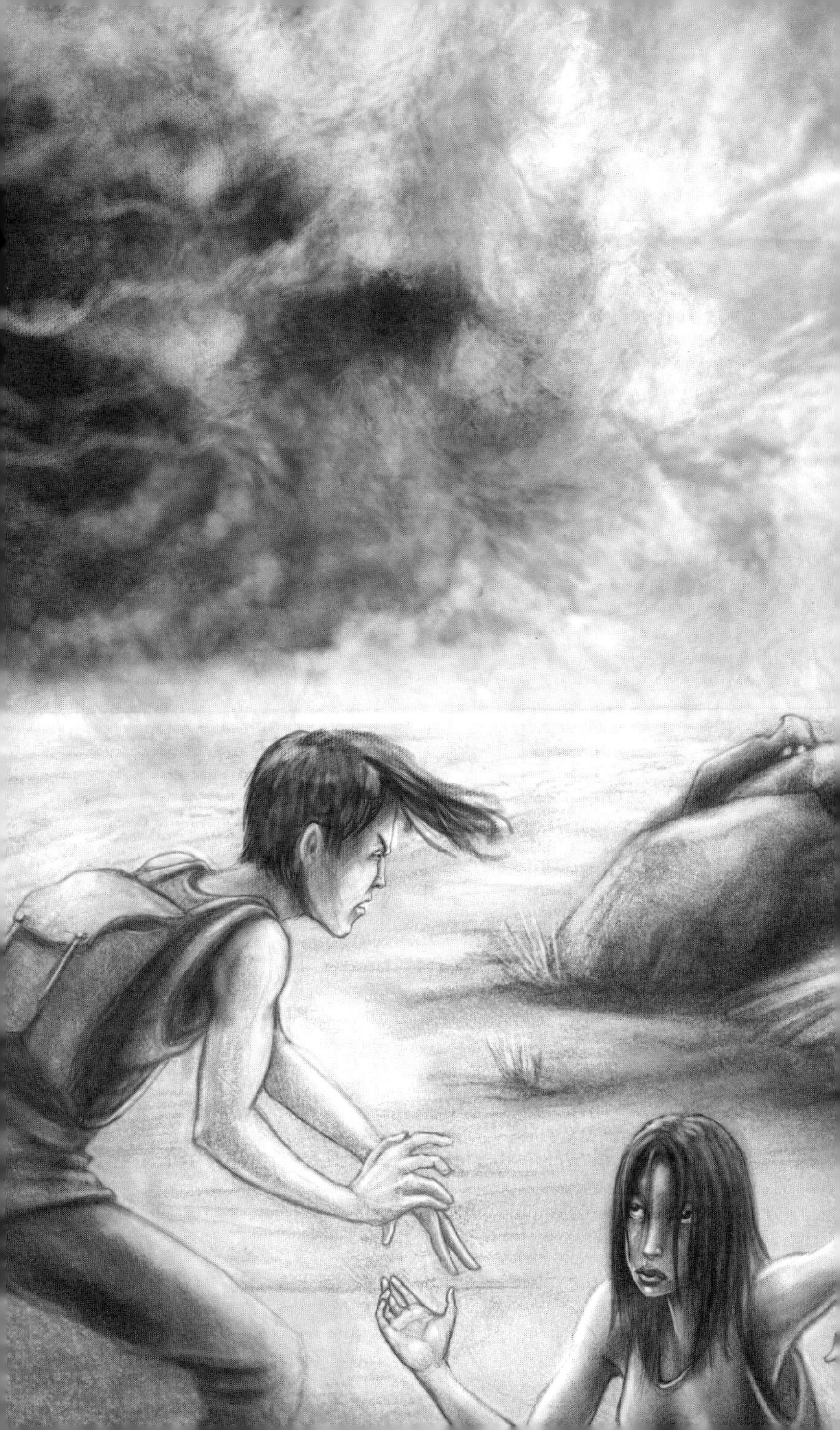

The Dark Man knows that the girl cannot walk any more.

All the time, the sky grows blacker and the waves grow bigger.

The Dark Man takes her into his arms. He will have to carry her, or the gray figure will soon catch them.

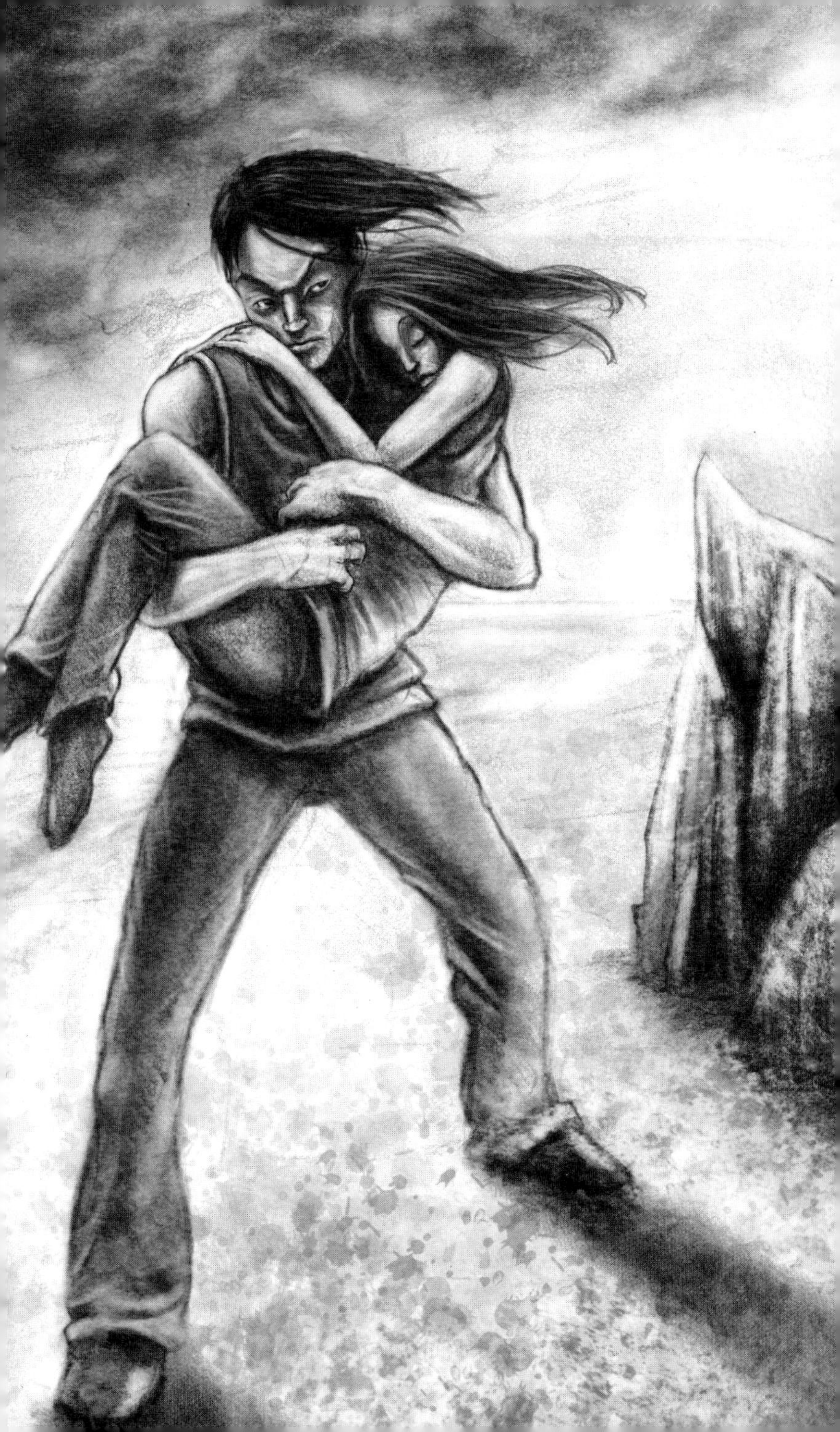

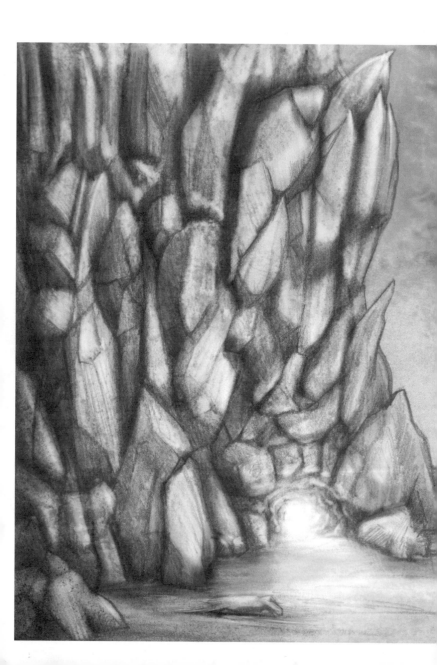

At the foot of the cliff, the Dark Man sees a yellow light. It comes from inside a small cave.

The girl sleeps in his arms, as he heads towards it.

At the entrance to the cave, he sees a figure waving him closer. It is a hermit holding a lamp.

"Here, quickly," the hermit says.

The Dark Man carries the girl into the cave.

"I have sealed the entrance with magic," the hermit says. "Someone is following you."

"I know," the Dark Man says, laying the girl on the ground. "But helping her is important. She is very weak."

A scream makes them turn to the cave entrance.

They see the gray figure. The Dark Man can see that it is a Shadow Master.

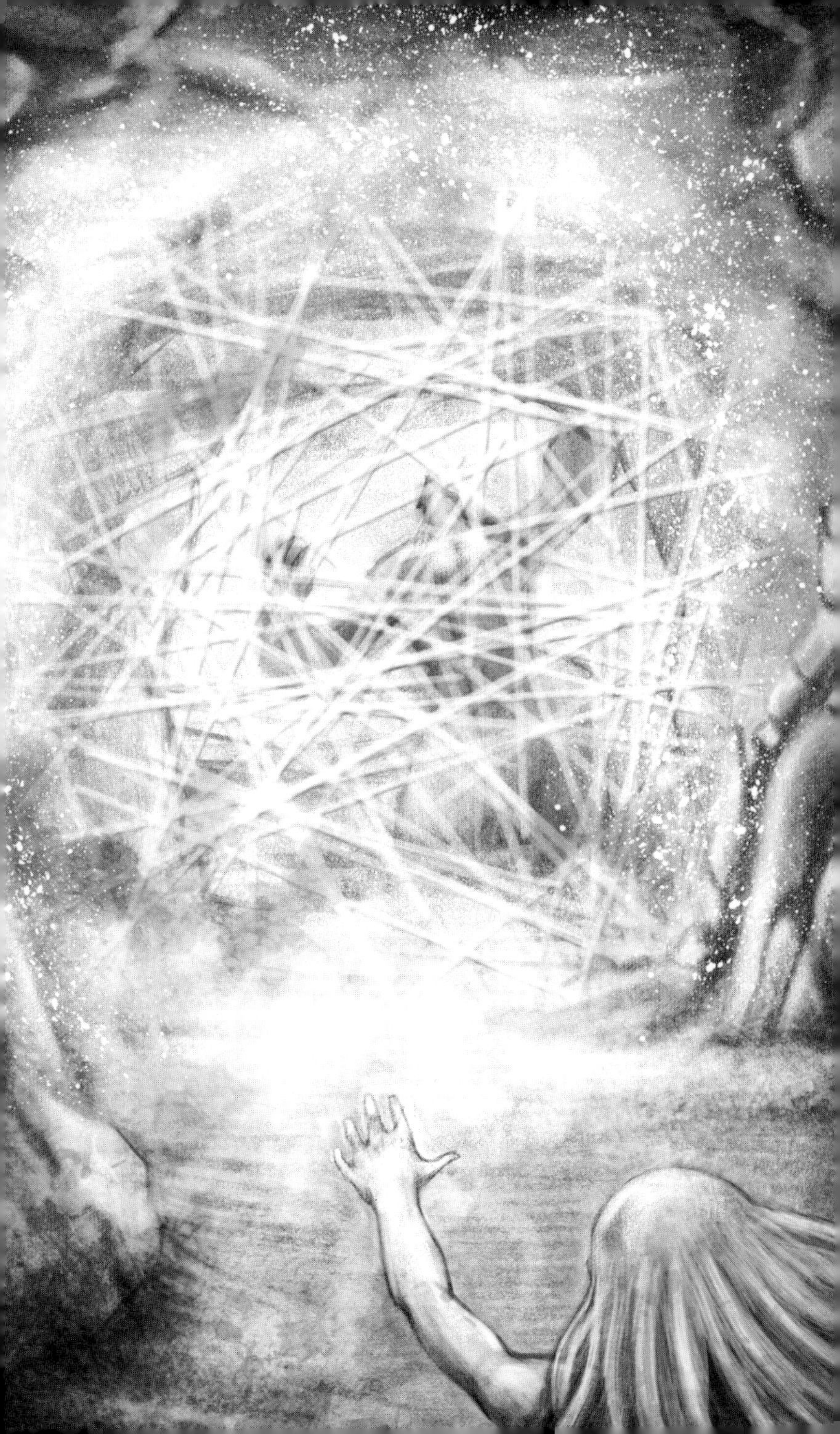

The Shadow Master cannot enter.

"The magic won't hold him for long," the hermit says.

Then he points to the girl.

"Is she ready for the light of the Dark Candle?"

"Her need is true," the Dark Man says.

Then he turns to the cave entrance, where the Shadow Master is casting a spell.

"I will keep him back."

Chapter Four:
In the Cave

The hermit carries the girl to the back of the cave.

On a ledge, there is a small, black candle.

The hermit lights the candle and the whole cave is suddenly dark. The candle has sucked all the light into itself.

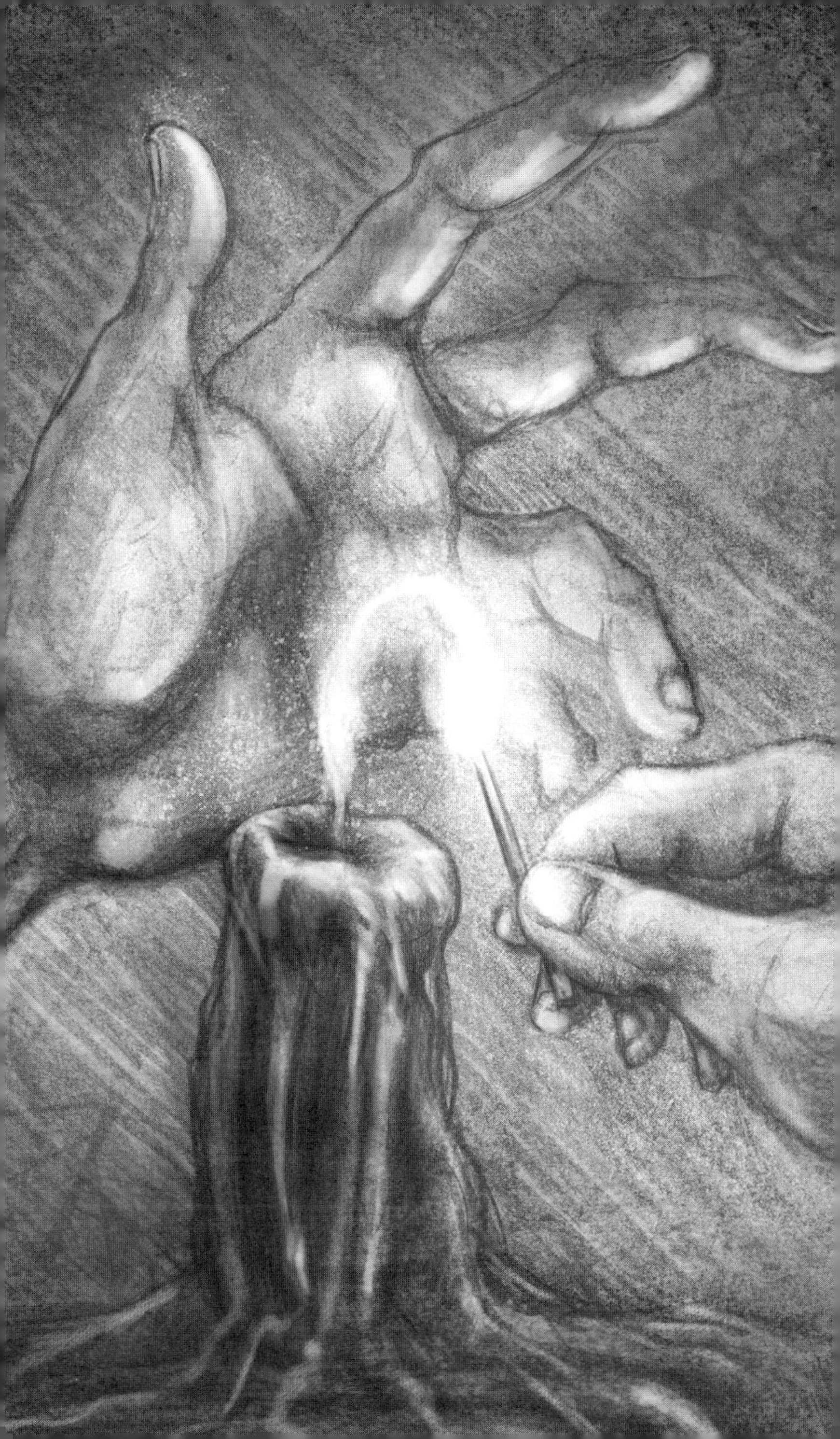

Then a soft yellow glow comes from the flame and flows over the girl.

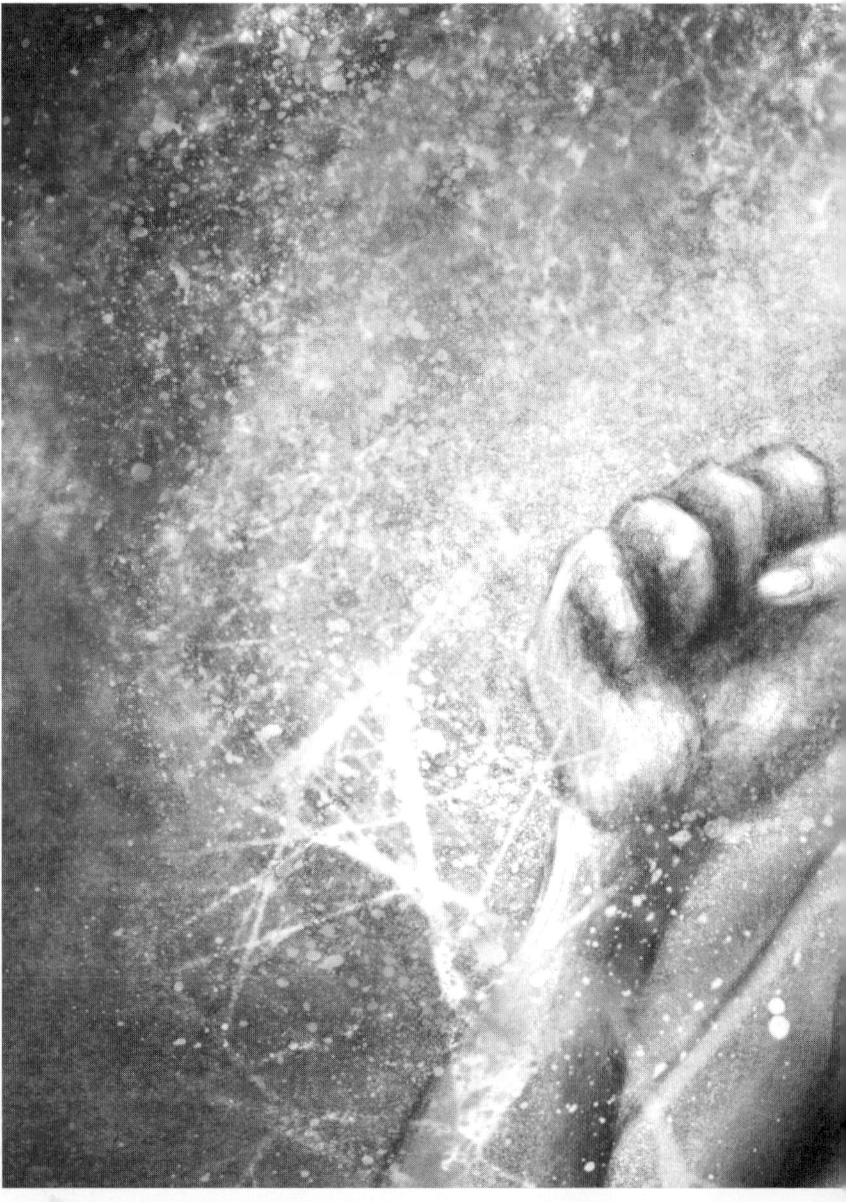

She cries out and then she sighs, as specks of glowing light sparkle on her skin.

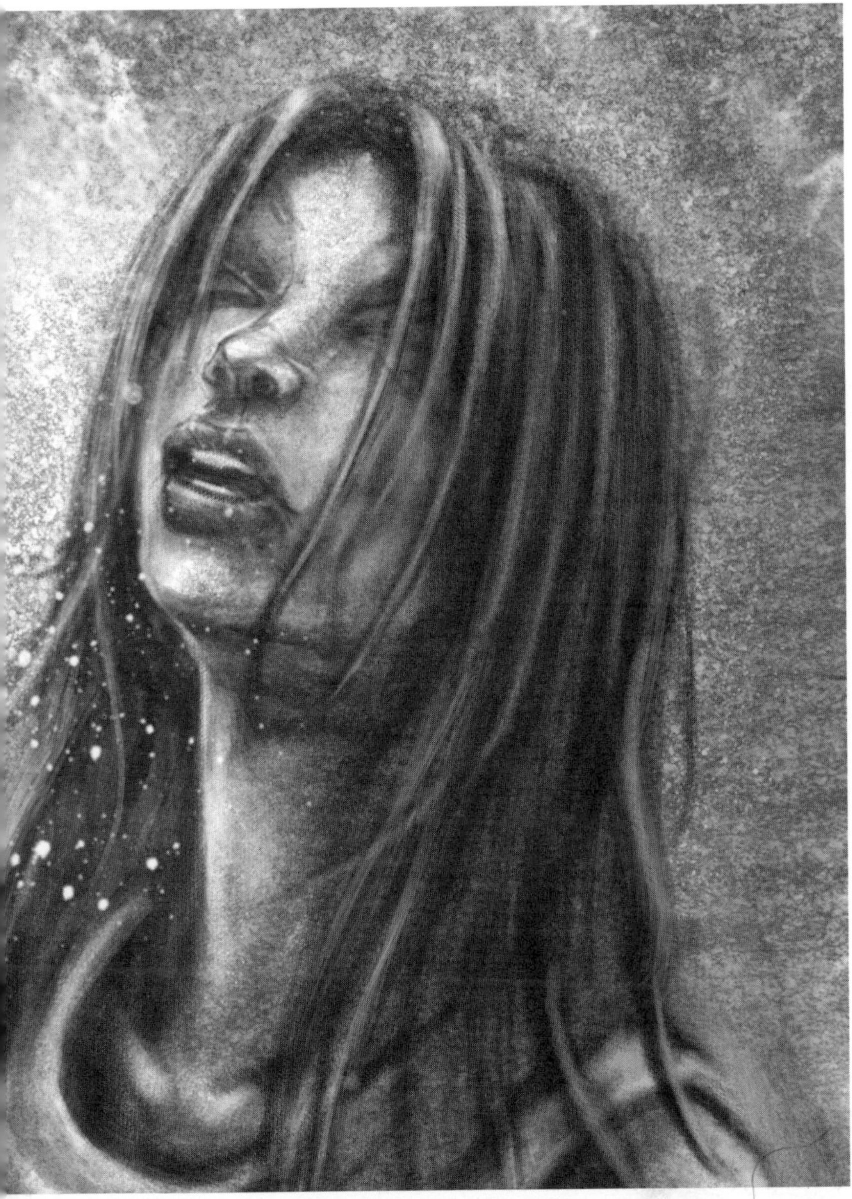

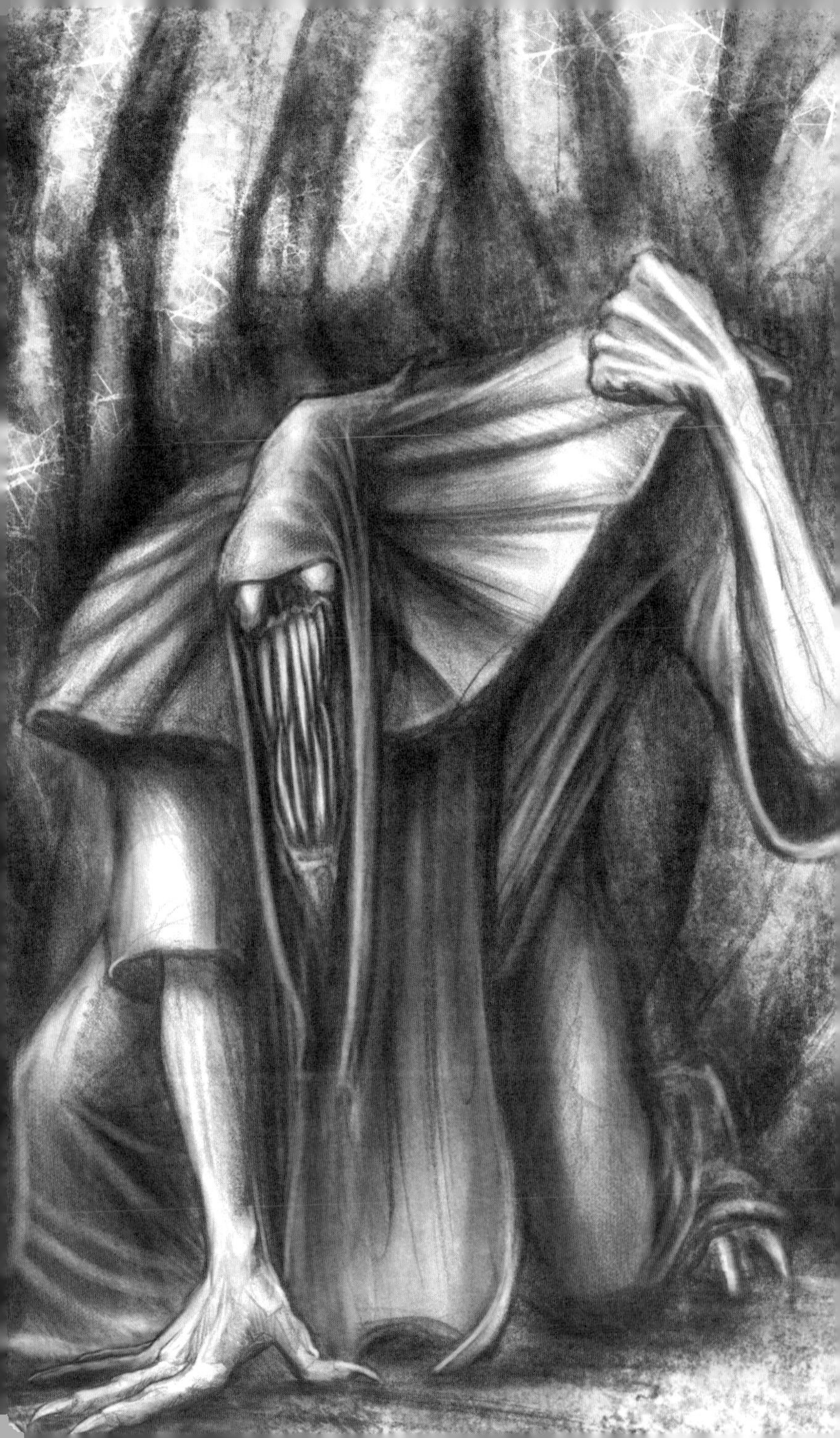

A roar comes from the mouth of the cave.

The Shadow Master has entered.

He leaps at the Dark Man, but the Dark Man steps to one side.

The Shadow Master stumbles into the candle's glow and screams.

The Dark Man rushes over to protect the girl.

In the candle's glow, the Shadow Master's skin becomes blistered and raw.

He is turning into a demon.

Then there is a loud bang and a flash of light.

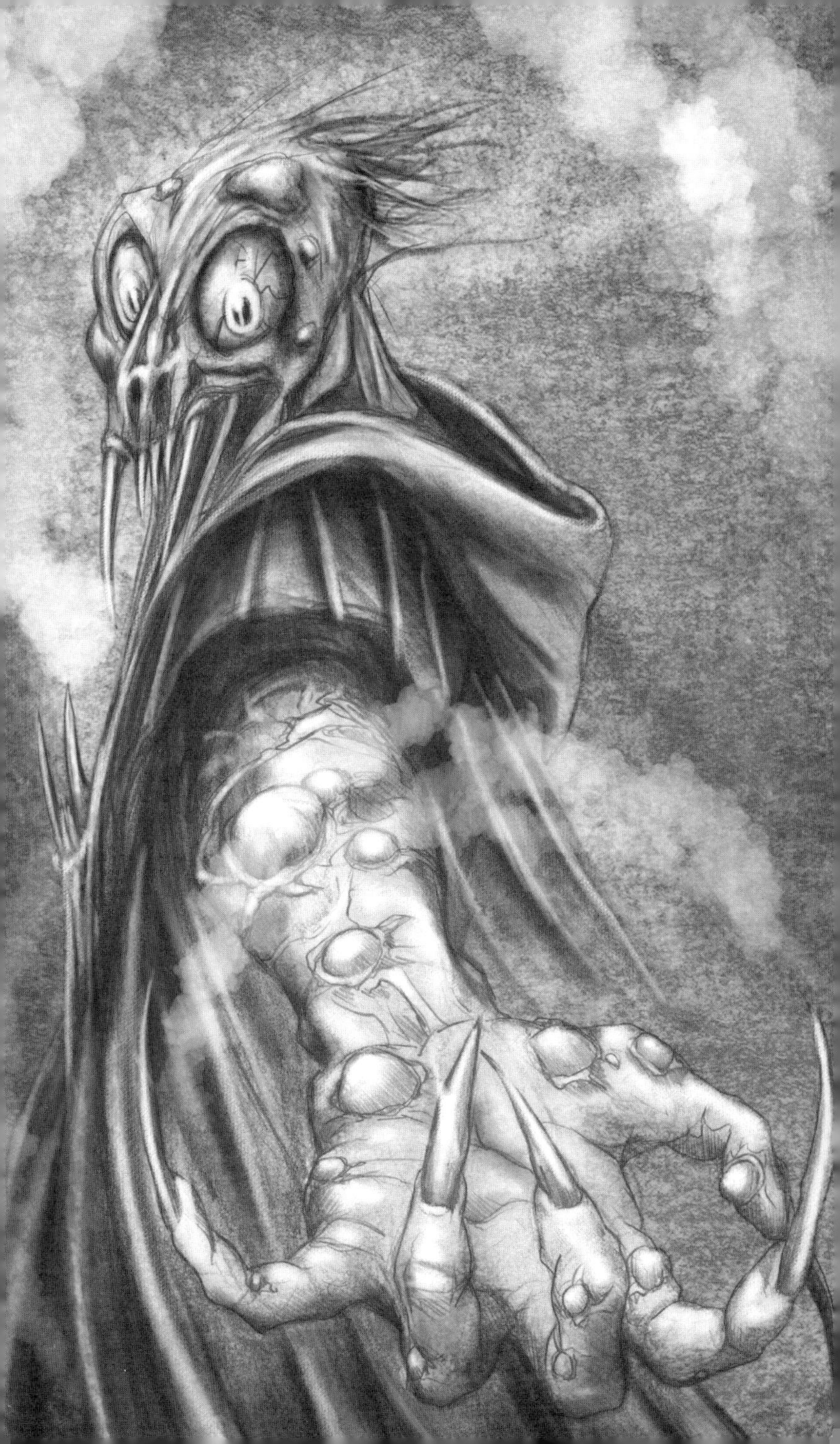

The Dark Man opens his eyes.

He is lying on the beach, but the ocean is gentle and the clouds are bright.

The girl kneels beside him.

"Did we find the Dark Candle?" she asks.
"I woke up and we were just lying here."

The Dark Man gets to his knees.

He can remember what happened in the cave.

He looks over to the cliff, but the cave has gone. He holds the girl in his arms.

"How do you feel?" the Dark Man asks.

"Like I could run all the way back to the city," she says.

The Dark Man helps her to her feet.

"Then we must have found the Dark Candle," he says, as they turn and head back to the city.

THE AUTHOR

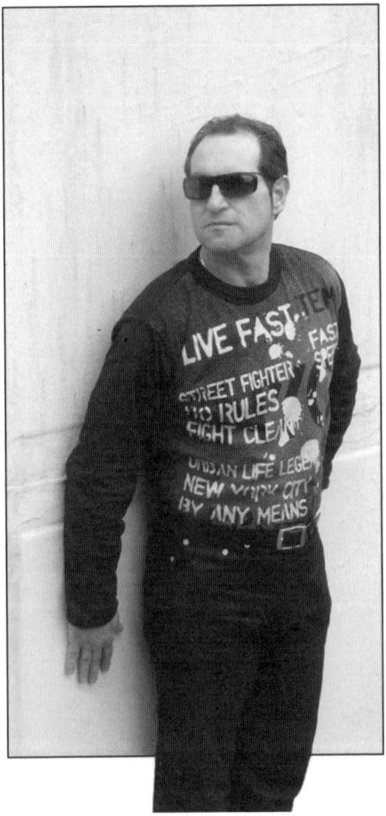
LIVE FAST
STREET FIGHTER
RULES
NEW
BY ANY MEANS

photograph: Rachel Ottewill

Peter Lancett is a writer, fiction editor, and film maker living and working in New Zealand and sometimes Los Angeles. He claims that one day he'll "settle down and get a proper job."